BLACK GHOSTS

Jail; it's nowhere anyone wants to go, where no one expects to go. I am prisoner 1858 formerly known as John Smith I am sitting on my cot in my cell listening to the sounds of the other prisoners and guards, the odor of jail is like no other, I just keep starting at my feet, and still cannot believe I was sent here. My family has been pulling the same scam for years without getting caught, I usually am very cautious, but then again I knew that my days were numbered. Hey, even the poor have to try to make ends meet. My family and I are sort of infamous, we find something someone has lost or been stolen and try to return it for a finders fee, but not this time. I was trying to help my good friend Peter Brown out. Of course I wanted to be compensated for my troubles. It was an easy job or at least it sounded easy, almost too easy that should have been a clue not to do it. I was distracted, that is my story and I am sticking to it, I was, thinking about asking my two girlfriends to marry me, there was no law saying that I could not have multiple wives, and beside I could not tell the Kirby twins apart.

There are some who say that whatever he family has found they must have stolen it, and in some case that was true I do have to admit that, but not this time. The judge had sentenced me to three years in jail for stealing a gold necklace my friend Peter had given to me to return for half the finder's fee. Little did I know the significance of this necklace, he never gave me the inside info he should have. Perhaps then I would not be sitting here, alone, thinking about how I, a part time scammer was finally scammed. Pete had

done it, good for him but he didn't think I would end up here. Peter thought that at least Queen Sandy would be happy to get her family necklace back; after all it was an heirloom but what he failed to mention to me is that it had been missing for three years. Needless to say she was not that appreciative and when I tried to tell her that I did not steal it because I was on a different planet when it went missing, I was just laughed at and called a liar and a thief.

For the first six months of my stay in his jail the only visitor beside my jailers was a female Black Ghost or at least that is what he called her because she was always dressed in black. I had always heard that ghosts were dressed in white or had a white glow to them, but this ghost was different and I could not make out her face due to the shadows she hide in. She seemed to float though walls at will and always at different times of the day or night, or she would just disappear altogether. Sometimes when alone in my cell she would appear and I would feel a cold draft or chill in the air that was how I could tell when she was hanging around my cell after a while. She seemed friendly for a ghost; she was curious and would ask me about where my ship was or my home. I didn't know what truths I should tell a ghost, would she be able to know if I was lying? But one strange question did come up in my conversations with her, and that question was why everyone called my family the King and/or Queen if thieves. That deserved a good answer and since I was the first member of my family to ever spend any time in a jail cell for longer then just a few days, I had really no good answer for her. At twenty-five I felt I was getting to old for this kind of work, it was no longer a game like it was in my younger years I needed to find another line of work, and hated being in jail.

From the only window in his cell he can just barely make out if it was night or day most of time, the window was so high up in my jail cell and was so very small I could not get a very good look outside.

Today all I could see was some smoke out the window then I heard some very loud explosions, so loud in fact that the shook the building. Some of the explosions today sounded very near the jail and this went though the late evening and into the next morning. Standing back a bit and looking up at the window I though he saw at least two space ships fly by firing their weapons at something or someone close by, it was followed by some very loud explosions that really trembled the building so hard it actually knocked me on to my ass a few times.

Suddenly I felt the cold air around me and then heard the Black Ghost speak from behind me, "*You are looking in the wrong direction for your freedom.*" I turned around as fast as I could, and after being knocked down again I looked up from the ground I was laying on and saw the Black Ghost standing by my cell door that now was wide open, she had one arm pointing at the open doorway. "*Go to your ship and leave this planet there is something waiting for you on your ship, take it some place safe until I tell you different, if you want to live that is.*" Then like always, she disappeared into thin air.

I stood back up and got my footing, then slowly headed toward the open cell door I am not sure if this is some kind of trap so I stopped short of the opening and looked back and forth up and down the cell blocks. When I did not see anyone else, he moved out into the hallway and quietly moved down past the cellblocks, then quickly toward the front of the building. Once I neared the end of the hallway and

came to the front I spotted one of the guards, he was sitting at his deck and looked terrified. He was holding his throat with both of his hands and his eyes were open wide he looked as if he was strangling himself, hmm how can that be, maybe I don't want to know. I moved a bit closer and could tell that he had died in front of me, he was no longer a threat so I crept up to him and took his blaster just in case I needed it, I knew he wouldn't need it anymore. Then I headed toward the front of the jailhouse and freedom or so I hoped. Once outside I saw what looked like a war was going on. Many things were in fames and space ships were flying around firing their weapons toward the ground striking buildings. There were other ships in the air in a dogfight. I didn't see anyone else outside of the jailhouse so I kept as close to some of the ruined buildings for cover and make my way down the street. I sure hope they didn't find my ship; I hid it in a pretty good place just outside of the city limits in an old abandoned barn. At least that is where I left it when I came to this God forsaken Planet

It took me over two hours to reach the old abandoned farm that I had found over six months ago, hopefully my ship is still intact. I had the blaster in my hand gripped firmly and I slowly approached the old barn quietly and quickly. I didn't dare get caught and be once again reacquainted with my cell. I had no idea what awaited me, and I needed to get off this damn planet. I slowly looked around and into the open door to the barn; yea a smile came over me, what of it? I saw I saw my ship was right where I left it, still was covered in hay from top to bottom so no one could see it if they just glanced into the barn. Really if

you had not known it was there you wouldn't even bat an eye or take a second look it was that well camouflaged with hay. Not a bad job I might say.
I opened the doors to the barn and looked back over my shoulder just to make sure I was not being followed, I now could see that the city was under attack from the air and some ground forces were moving in.

I moved rapidly toward the backside of my ship, my plan was to remove just enough hay necessary for lift off, just in case some intruder decided to show his ugly face. But once around the back not visible from the door I stopped dead in my tracks. The hatch to my ship was uncovered and wide open, so now I moved in close and real quiet like toward my ship and pointed the blaster in toward the open hatch. I slowly stepped into the open hatch and looked around, I took a deep breath and relaxed my grip because I didn't see anyone or anything unusual or out of place. Then I headed straight toward the cockpit. Once in the cockpit I closed the door to the cockpit off from the rest of the ship, and locked it just in case someone was in the back of the ship hiding from me.

I took a seat in the captain's chair and strapped myself in. Then I closed the hatch to the ship and started take off procedures, turning on the engines. My ship was still covered in hay but as I started to get forward momentum the hay started to fall off and I crept out of the old barn. I took one last look toward the city, the fires, the mayhem, then lifted the ship off of the ground and pointed it sky ward and basted off that damn planet fast. Half way into space I looked out my window and thought I saw someone shooting at me, a bright light shot by my window and it was

either a real close call or I was hit somewhere because my ship shook a bit, and I felt it.

I didn't breathe easy until I was in space and away from that nightmare I called home for a bet. I then set a course for his home planet of Ares, but also avoided using highly patrolled areas just case someone was chasing me, no one was going to follow me to my home planet today. I checked my instruments to see if there was any damage to my ship. I didn't see anything out of the ordinary so I turned on the gravity and inclined my chair back a bit starting to relax a bit. I looked around the cockpit, and then started to think about the Black Ghost. What did she want me to take with me, where was it, and why did she want me to take it to my home planet to take care of for her?

I unstrapped myself from the captain's chair and got up, I decided to scope out the ship and go find out what my Black Ghost had in store for me and where could it be on my ship?

I unlocked the door to the cockpit and opened it up, but then what I saw stopped me cold, about five feet from the door was a young girl dressed in rags. I was guessing she was between the ages of seventeen and nineteen years old. As soon as she saw me, she dropped to her knees with her hands out in front of herself on the floor and her head down.

I just looked down at this young girl, I am puzzled and probably have a shocked look on my face, I took one small step closer to her, and I didn't want to scare her off, "Who are you? What are you doing on my ship?"

She wouldn't look up at me, "I'm called Sarah and my Mistress ordered me to go to your ship and wait for your orders, Sir!"

I bent down a bit and put my hands on my knees, I wanted to get a closer look, I just shook my head a few times I tried to look into her eyes as if all the answers were there, but she wouldn't budges, "Who was your Mistress?"

She still kept her head down and would not look up at me, she especially would not make any eye contact, "I have never seen her sir just heard her voice, I have sensed her since I was five years old when my mom sold me to her to be her servant and she was always dressed in black, I never got a good look at her face."

I was stunned, was she talking about the same Ghost that I knew? I was still shaking my head in disbelief, I knew it was risky but could not stand it anymore, so I reached out and took Sarah by her shoulders and picked her up slightly, "Stand up and look at me."

Sarah slowly stood up but kept her head down, and she shook her head no, "That would be wrong my Master as a Slave cannot look at his or her Master's, it is the law."

I took a step back; astonishment was written all over my face, "You are not my slave! Who said you were to be my slave?"

"But Master, my Mistress has ordered me to serve you until she calls me back into her services." As Sarah answered me she kind of peeked around to take a look at my ship, still without looking up at my face.

I reached out and gently embraced Sarah's chin with my right hand. I proceeded to tilt her head up, until I was looking right into her eyes. "Look at me." I demanded.

Sarah shyly took a step back away from me and kept her head down, then turned her back to me, "It is forbidden for me to look at my Master face, Sir."

I could not believe what Sarah was wearing, it disturbed me, she had only on filthy clothes and they hung on her like rags I used to wipe my hands when repairing my ship. She had blond hair and even her hair was unclean too as if she had not bathed in a very long time. "When was the last time you bathed, washed your hair or had clean clothes?"

Sarah slowly turned back toward me, but never lifted her head, I was beginning think she was stuck that way "Two weeks ago, Master, my Mistress did not like it when I bathed too often, she did not like it when I was too clean, Sir, I never asked why."

I put both of my hands up to her face and shook my head back and forth a few time, then pointed toward the back of his ship, "There is a shower back there, go and use it. I will find you some clean clothes to wear while you do that, when you're with me you will bathe once a day and wear clean clothes, do you hear me?"

She then Bowed to me before she turned and headed toward the back of the ship, I also noted that it looked like she had not eaten much either and she was very thin, but I couldn't tell really, because of the way her clothing hung on her. I still was shaking my head as I walked into my small sleeping quarters. I started at the drawers opening some drawers and pulling out some clothes that I thought would come as close as I could get to fitting her or at least would be clean and fit her better than her current clothing. I took the clothes in hand and walked over to the bathroom and heard the shower going I opened the door a bit, just enough to put the clothes in, I didn't want to startle her so I did it real quiet like. I never needed to have a lock on my bathroom, I never intended for anyone but me on this ship, of course that would have to change if I married the Kirby twins I would definitely have to

make changes in the living quarters, and the sleeping area was not big enough. I stuck the clean items though the open door and laid them down on a counter top and without surprising her just spoke from outside the door, "I laid out some clean clothes that I think will fit you. Make sure you use that soap bar and scrub your head too." I closed the door gently pleased with myself had a little smile on my face. I then headed to the kitchen to make something for the both of us to eat, I couldn't help but feel like someone was watching me at all times, hmm it was disturbing and something to not, but looking around the ship and not seeing anyone I just shook it off, it had to be the stress, or the uneasiness of having someone on board.

I opened one of the storage lockers in the kitchen, and hoped I had enough food for two people to eat until I got back home, I never thought of this contingency when stocking supplies on my ship. Of course a day or so was not a problem, the Kirby twins had spent time on his ship but that was a couple years ago, and only for two days and what a couple evenings that was not bragging or anything, but that was not in space but on the planet and I had a way to get more food if need.

I pulled out two frozen meals and put them in the oven, then I started to wonder what the heck I was going to tell my family about Sarah when I reached home. Suddenly I started thinking about other things I would have to adjust around the ship like what I was going to do about sleeping arrangements. My quarters were small and I don't think Sarah would want to share a bed with her Master that was obvious. Sarah was finished with her shower and now standing in front of me with her hand still down. She was now wearing the clothes I had given her and they did not fit

her thin frame very well but at least they were in one piece and clean, she didn't look very happy about wearing them though.

Sarah was not sure why her Mistress wanted her to go with me, and she started to tell me some things her Mistress had said to her on the planet. Sarah was just told to go to my ship and hide on it and leave with me. Then she was told to do whatever I told her to do and be subservient to me because I was going to be her new Master until she had called her back into her services again. She said that she had never worn clean clothes before, because her Mistress did not want her to stand out in a crowd, especially while doing her Mistresses bidding at that time for her.

I just walked up to Sarah and put my right hand on her left shoulder, "I have started cooking something for us to eat, and I'm hungry how about you?" I then turned toward the over and opened a cabinet taking out a couple of plates and set them on a small table. As I was doing that and setting the table I realized that Sarah was getting ready to take the food out of the oven. The timer went off so she proceeded to remove the food and set it onto the small table I had just set. After that she did the weirdest thing, she never lifting her head and took two steps back and stood there. I then realized that she was waiting for me to sit down at the table and eat first.

I just rolled his eyes into the back of my head. I couldn't get used to this Master Slave relationship at all, sternly I just had to have a talking to her and set things right, "As long as we are together, we will eat together and at the same table at the same time do you hear me?"

Sarah did not understand my demands, this was going to be harder then what I thought, "But Master it

is not right for me to eat with you, and you must eat first then me, it is the law, sir."

I crossed my arms across my cheat and continued, "That is another thing you do not call me your Master my name is John. Now sit down and EAT THIS INSTANT! I do not care about you law!" I sat down and started to eat my food without looking up at the girl.

She was not sure what to do at this point, all of her life she has served others including eating alone, and especially never with her Mistress. She slowly took a seat at the table, but still would not look at me, she looked lost, but she began slowly to eat her food not speaking a word.

I waited a few minutes for her to become comfortable with the idea first, then observed her after a few bites at least she was eating her food but still wouldn't look at me while at the table. I was finishing up my meal when I leaned back a bit and looked at her square on; I needed answers, "Tell me about your Mistress?"

Sarah put down her fork and took a deep breath, "She always wore black, I could never see her face and she sometimes looked like she could walk through walls or she would just disappear into thin air. She sent me to listen in on people at different times and places and then report back to her on what I heard or saw. Something she had me pick something up and bring it to her or give it to someone ease."

As I was listening to her I stood up and picked up my plate and put it in the sink and then turned back toward her, "When you are done eating, you can go and sleep in my quarters, I will sleep in the cockpit until we get where we are going."

The girl looked up at me for just a moment and then bowed her head once again, "Master, I mean John, you can have the bed I will sleep on the floor, next to your bed it is not right that I take your bed, sir."

I closed my eyes for a second and then gave her a very stern look, "As long as you are with me, you will sleep in a bed and not on the floor you hear me!" I didn't wait for a response; frankly I was tried of the idea all together, so I just headed toward the bridge, I was angry and upset about what she and told me about her Mistress. Her Mistress must be my Black Ghost I met in my cell I started wondering what she was up to and why she sent Sarah to me. I mean I didn't need a servant and why was she so important. In my line of work it was best to work alone just in case I were to end up getting caught like this time and spending a long time in jail like I was supposed to. I mean what were to happen if I did have to spend a couple years behind bars. I sat down in the captain's chair and stared out the window into space, I was thinking what did I do that could have caused me to be put into that cell, I didn't do anything wrong, I had an alibi and still ended up there, something was wrong. When I get home I am going to have a long talk with my old pal Peter about that necklace he gave me to return. I looked back over my shoulder because I could not shake this feeling that someone was watching me again so I got up and looked around the bridge for a bit, but again I didn't find anyone hiding anywhere I must be going crazy, or maybe I am a bit paranoid since being in jail.

I started to head back to the front of the bridge when I spotted Sarah standing in the doorway, not lifting her head yet, wow, it was really beginning to wear on my nerves. I walked up to her and reached

my hand out to put under her chin, but she took a step back before I could do so, "Is there anything ease I can do for you today, John?"

I gave her a little smile, "No I don't need anything and if I did I am capable to get it myself, so you can go to bed, we will be reaching my home planet later tomorrow, unless something comes up before we get there."

She turned around and promptly walked back to the sleeping quarters before she got into bed she felt a hand on her shoulder and she stopped in her tracks, *"Stay close to him at all time, listen to what he says and do want he tell you to do."* Feeling the hand let go of her shoulder she walked to the bed and lay down and just stared up at the ceiling soon she fell asleep.

I got up out of the captain's chair took a blanket out of a storage bin and covered myself up as I sat back down. I stared out the window at the stars and then fell asleep too.

The next morning I was in the kitchen getting some breakfast for the both of us to eat when I spotted Sarah standing in the doorway to the sleeping quarters, she looked sad and a bit lost. Just like the day before she has her head down a bit and she may have been crying because her eyes were red from what I could see, and she has put her old clothes back on. I walked over and stopping a few feet from her I was more puzzled then angry at this point, "What is wrong? Why have you put these clothes back on?"

Sarah took one small step toward me, "I do not know what I'm supposed to do and I do not feel right wearing your good clothes."

I put my hands on his hips, yea I was right she was lost and confused "I want you to wear them until we can find you something that fits you better and I wanted you to throw these old clothes away, you don't need them anymore. As to what your purpose is and what that has to do with me, that is something we need to talk about I have never had anyone help me in my line of business before and I don't need a servant." I reached out to Sarah and turned her around and then pushed her back toward the sleeping quarters. I watched her slowly head back to the quarters I then returned to the kitchenette and continued getting food prepared for them to eat.

Sarah returned to the room and put on the clothes I gave her. After taking off her old ones and saw a mirror on the wall so she walked over and looked at herself in it. It has been a very long time since she last wore anything this good or slept in a bed, her Mistress never gave her anything but rags to wear and never let her sleep in a bed before. She wished that her Mistress had told her what she expected from her with this John it looked like he did not need any help so her purpose was unclear but she trusted her Mistress to take good care of her nonetheless.

I put the food on the table and saw the girl return to the kitchen. For the first time I came to the realization that she was kind of cute, she had cleaned up good, even if the clothes didn't quite fit. I had already eaten but waited at the table until Sarah had seated herself and started to eat, "I have never had any help before and I'm not sure I need any help, but I will try to accept that. I kind of like the idea of having someone around to help me."

She looked down at her food, "I will do whatever you ask me to do, John."

Without another word I got up and headed back to the cockpit, I had to sync my ship's projection to my home world's arrival, timing was everything. It was not safe to come home in the middle of the night, my father did not like to be woken up he loved his sleep. Once I had synced the ship's speed so I would be landing in the late morning, my mind went elsewhere like trying to figure out why my Black Ghost's wanted me to have Sarah with me? My father and the rest of his family had always worked alone, it was easier and you did not have to worry about anyone ease getting hurt or arrested. Being in a family that finds things and returns them to their owners was not easy work. We had always worked alone and all had our own resources for finding missing or stolen things that needed to be returned for a finder's fee.

One of the first things I was going to do was have a long talk with Peter about where he got that necklace and whom he got it from. It would be the first time I had ever asked where the stuff came from. Peter may not like what I had to say, I was not a violent person but there was always a first time. I took my seat back into the captain's chair and sat looking out the window at the stars my memories seemed like a bad dream and I returned to thinking about the cause of my imprisonment and all I could think of was that the King wanted to make a example of me and send a message to the rest of my family. I quickly sent out a message to my father that I was returning home soon and I had someone with me, but I didn't tell him who it was, how she ended up on my ship or why I had her, I just was not sure what to say about Sarah yet. I looked over my shoulder and saw that Sarah was walking toward him well she is nice kid and for some reason I was beginning to like her. I made a gesture to the co-

pilot seat next to me. "Have a seat we will be landing in an hour and I need to tell you a few things first. When you meet my family, do not keep your head down, look right at them, they just would not understand the whole servant thing and I am not ready to explain. Do not tell them anything unless they asked you something and always tell them the truth." I looked back out the window for a moment and then back at Sarah, "I'm going to have my sister Lisa help you shop for some new clothes, not more rags, I want you to always wear clean clothes as long as you are with me."

Sarah looked out the window from the co-pilot seat, she has never been in space before and it kind of scared her but also intrigued her at the same time. She then turned toward me and gave me a little smile, that was a first and I noticed her beauty when she did. I couldn't believe she was a servant, "I have never had nice clothes or slept in a bed before I was on your ship." She then went to gazing out the window again, she was watching intensely as she saw the planet starting to get bigger and bigger as they approached it.

I started to engage the control panel getting the ship ready to land on my home planet, I again had memories of my time in the cell, I still can't put my finger on why this Black Ghost wanted me to have Sarah with me and why me of all people.

I looked at the time on the control panel and saw that it was early morning on the planet and I would be met at the landing area by my family, it had been a while since I was home. I headed the ship downward toward the surface of the planet and then smiled at the girl, "Better put the straps on sometimes it can get a little rough when landing." I put on my own straps and looked out of the corner of he eye and watched Sarah slowly doing the same.

Within a few minutes the ship was heading toward the landing area I sent a message out to the base that I was coming in for a landing and told them to relate to my family that I would be landing in about five minutes. Sarah was still continuously looking out the window, her eyes open wide as she saw that there were a lot of green trees and fields with crops growing tall in them. She could also see what looked like a small town near a small lake; she was surprised and a little anxious to see it up close.

I flew around the town and waited for the main hanger doors to open so I could fly in and land, there was not any place to just land a ship that came here to do business.

When I saw that the hanger doors were starting to open I slowed the ship down and headed toward the hanger. As I got closer I spotted two people standing near the open doors and I entered the hanger to land. When I was beginning to put the landing gear down I saw that both of the men who were standing there were armed, this is something I have never seen here before. After I landed I looked around the hanger he saw about five other ships in it, only one was being worked on and two look like they many have been in some kind fight. I smiled at the girl; "This does not look good so stay close to me until I find out what is going on here." I unstrapped myself from the captain's chair and stood up heading toward the back hatch to the outside of the ship.

Sarah also unstrapped herself and took a peak outside. She saw one of the armed men heading toward the ship and he had his weapon drawn and at

the ready. She turned around and followed close by John toward the main hatch. She looked concerned, and was scared not only for herself but also for me now as well.

I opened the hatch and is met by someone he didn't know and he was pointing his blaster at me he looked uncompromising and I knew whatever I said to him would not change the situation, he now saw Sarah standing behind him. "Both of you keep your hands where I can see them at all times if you want to live that is, or else you are going to have a really bad day!"

I raised both of his hands, "Can I asks what is going on here?"

He waving the blaster a bit at us to walk in front of him, "Keep quite until you see the boss."

The girl and I gradually exited the ship and kept our hands up about chest level. We headed toward the doorway that led out of the hanger. I took a glance around he saw that even the people working on the ships were wearing blaster on their hips and I didn't recognize any of them.

One of the men who was working on the one ship suddenly thought he felt a cold breeze as the doors to the hanger where closing and it felt strange there was no wind outside today.

At gunpoint we walked into the hallway and headed toward my father's office, I saw few people that I knew and every one of them were all armed as well. I didn't have a good feeling about this. I followed the man as instructed until we were at my father's office. I was shock when I saw two armed men standing on each side of the door to the office, what was this all about?

One of the men opened the door and waved them in with the blaster he was holding and we proceeded to enter into my father office.

Once inside I saw that my dad Frank and two of my uncles, Tom and Jack and three other men were seated at a table. They looked like they had been arguing over something and were not reaching a conclusion any time soon. I looking at Sarah who looked frightened so I whispered to her, *"Stay close to me, I won't let anything happen to you."*

When my father Frank saw me in the doorway he stood up and his jaw dropped to the floor, he then moved around the table rapidly and walked up to me grasping my arms and giving me a big hug, when he pulled away I could see that he had tear in his eyes. "I thought I would never see you again, we heard they jailed you and you would not be getting out any time soon. When I got your message I was over joyed that you were free and on your way here."

I looked at his father and then at my uncles and then asked my father and the other men, "What is going on here?"

My father then put his right hand on my left shoulder he looked at me sadly, "The raider have a new leader and he is a power hunger S.O.B., he has been attacking other planets and enslaving the people or kidnapping them for ransom. They have attacked us twice in the last two months that is why everyone here is armed now and on edge." My father then turned to face me and finally spotted Sarah for the first time, who was trying to hide behind my back, "Who is this beautiful woman, she looks a bit young for you if you asks me or are you looking for three wives' now?" My father then winked at me and giggled like a young schoolgirl. "Or have you forgotten about the Kirby Twins?"

I took a glance over my shoulder at Sarah and then decided to take a chance telling my father a story that

seemed incredibly farfetched, "Her name is Sarah and she worked for a well, I don't know how to say it any other way so here goes, a Black Ghost, who by the way got me out of my jail cell when the raider attacked the planet I was on and no I have not forgotten about my lovely Kirby twins."

My father Frank took two steps back and his face turned white, his mouth dropped open. I then looked at my uncles whose faces have also turned white. "I know what you're thinking, but I cannot make this shit up, I'm here aren't I? My father finally got his speech back, "Did you say Black Ghost? Was it a female Black Ghost?"

I slowly looked around at everyone in the room then turned back toward my father whose eyes were wide like the doughnuts so neatly place on the table, "All I ever heard was a female voice, and she was always dressed in black. I never sew her face it was coved."

My uncle Jack slowly walked up next to my father Frank he had a look of terror on his face, "It's a good thing you did not see her face if you had, you would be dead! Anyone who looks at the face of a female Black Ghost dies a horrible death or so I have heard."

I looked at my uncle and father, "I do not understand what the Black Ghost are? She was the first one I have ever came into contact with or heard of."

My Uncle Tom approached his brothers and stood between them then tried to explain the origins of these ghosts the best that he could, "They are a sisterhood of females who use magic to gather information and what they do with it is any one guess. Just before you were born John, King Artie thought he found their secret hiding place and wiped them out. Well, it now looks like he was wrong, if you have seen one of them after

all of these years and there may be more of them still around."

Uncle Jack went around me and stood in front of Sarah and bent over a bit, "Tell me Sarah want kind of things did you do for your Black Ghost?"

Sarah slowly looked up at me and then back at my uncle, "My mistress had me go to places and listen to what people were talking about, she also had me pick up stuff for her and take it somewhere or give it to someone else. But mostly just listen in on different conversations and report back to her to tell her what I have heard."

My Uncle Jack turned and faced my father and my Uncle Tom then he then turned back and confronted Sarah, and me "Can you tell us some of the things you have heard?"

Sarah looked at me she was afraid to tell anyone anything because she didn't know what the Black Ghost would do, and I didn't blame her one bit she bit her lower lip pondering for a moment, and I could see her weighing out the situation, would she be in trouble since she was put into this situation and whose wrath was worse, she didn't know me or these people. Then she turned toward my uncle and explained but only generally speaking no names were given. "Who was dating whom? How some business people were doing, if what they were doing was benefiting to others and doing good thing or bad things. Sometimes finding out what other leaders were doing if what they were doing was corrupt or virtuous. My Mistress had me dress in dirty clothes so no one took note of me or cared that I was there." She then looked up at me with her eyes mournful on the cusp of tears and back at my Uncle Jack, "I do not know what else to tell you about my Mistress, sir."

Jack slowly walked back to the table and then sat down his face filled with worry then he looked up at me with apprehension, "If the Black Ghosts are back, it could mean they have something planned or are working on something and we may not like it."

Uncle Frank walked over to me and gave me a big hug now the hug wasn't one like from a loved one but one like a big old bear would give, I almost thought I would pass out for a moment, tears were flowing from his eyes, and "Its good to have you home again, my boy."

I returned Frank's hug but gave the old man a break and didn't squeeze the life out of him, then I took a step back and looked at the rest of them, "I need to find Peter Brown, could you tell me where he is I need to have a little chat with him?"

All of the men suddenly stopped speaking and just stared at me, I have to admit for a moment it was a little creepy my father slowly walked back up to me he had a strange look on his face, I'd seen that look before he needed to tell me something I didn't want to hear, "He is the new leader of the Raiders and he is very power hungry, those that follow him are more than crazy and really love to hurt people! There is a rumor that he is looking for the lost King and Queen Johnson of the Planet Temple who disappeared eighteen years ago, they had with them over a ten tons of gold and other gems, so they say."

I threw my arms up in the air shrugging my shoulders, "Everyone has been looking for that! But no one knows where to start looking. No one ever saw them leave Temple, they just disappeared without a trace one day, and I can't believe it."

Uncle Jack peered at me, my father Frank and Uncle Tom, "Many have looked all over Temple for

them the gold and gems, but have never found anything. Empty building where the gold and gems where once stored lay in ruins. Once someone did find what looked like a nursery next to the Queens room but it looked as if it was never used, so some think the Queen may have disappeared with a baby too. The room was pink and held an essence of a female presence so there may be a princess out there that no one knows about."

Tom slowly walked back to the table and sat back down he looked almost as if he had been defeated as he addressed the others, "If you ask me someone on Temple probably killed them and hide their bodies and there was undoubtedly never any gold or gems. I mean think about it, the talk of gold and gems was just a way to keep people from searching for the King and Queen's body, if they are really dead. No one can hide that much gold and gems without someone finding it."

I just took a deep breath and then looked back at Sarah and talked to my dad and uncles, "I do not care about the gold or the gem that is if there were any in the first place right now all I care about is that I'm home again and I'm free." Sarah was trying to stay behind me, "Uncle Tom, I would like to have Lisa take Sarah shopping for some good clothes the ones I gave her do not fit her very well." I wanted all of this to be over, I was tired and needed to eat a good meal, but I knew the questions were still coming.

Then one of the three other older men at the table stood up and took a few steps over toward me and Sarah he looked Sarah in the eyes, "How did you come to work with your Black Ghost?"

Sarah looked over at me hesitating to speak at first, she had been though a lot and was extremely timid, then she turned back and looked at the older man who

asked the question, "My mother sold me to her I think, sir. I never saw my mother or my father again."

My uncle Jack moved over toward him and put his hand on his shoulder, "Adam, we cannot go around being suspense of everyone who come here with one of our friends or family."

Adam turned and gave Jack a stern look, "I do not trust anyone who comes here after that last attack we had last month, they said they came to buy some crops from the farmers here but instead attacked us and stole the crops!"

My father Frank got between Adam and John and then turned and looked over at me and Sarah, "You have to understand we are at war with the Raiders and we have lost a lot of our good friends, and not just here on a few other planets as well over the last six months.

I shook my head in disbelief, "I have a hard time believing Peter has changed so much and become that ruthless!" I looked over at Sarah, she still looked frightened and so frail to me, "No more questions for now, so I'm asking again I would like Lisa to help Sarah get some new clothes to wear while she is living here."

A couple hours later Lisa was walking with Sarah through town window-shopping clothing stores and just like everyone else Lisa was armed with a blaster. I told Lisa to cool it for a while, Sarah had been though a lot today I told her not to ask too may questions, unless Sarah started to talk about things on her own. They decided one store looked promising so Lisa opened the door to the store and waited for Sarah to walk into it and followed. Sarah scoped the area out, she was nervous and her eyes were darting around the

room like she was looking for a place to hide, but at the same time listing to everything that is being said around them. She was used to that, listening and observing everything.

They both headed toward the female clothing area Lisa could see that Sarah had no undergarment so she picked up a bra and pantie set that she thought would fit Sarah and handed it to her. Sarah looked at it strangely, it was foreign to her she has never worn anything like that before. Lisa realized she was out of her element and took it out of Sarah's hand she just gave her a little smile, "Take your shirt off and let's see if this is the right size for you?"

Sarah just looked down at her feet and then started to pull off her shirt slowly and as she turned her back toward Lisa to put the bra on Lisa saw Sarah's back and a look of shock came over her face. All over Sarah's back was a large tattoo that showed some planets and moons with lines going between some of the planets, it covered Sarah's whole back.

With wide eyes, Lisa turned Sarah around, "Who put that on your back?"

Sarah looked over her shoulder as if trying to see what is on her back, "My mom and dad put it there just before I was sold to my Mistress and my dad said it was for my future. I have tried a few times to see what it is but I cannot see it very well. What is it?"

Lisa's eyes slowly scanned the area and then faced Sarah again, trying to look normal so she would not draw attention. "It something I want my dad to see when we get done shopping today, perhaps he can explain it better then I can, but let us pick up something to put on that covers it for now, just in case."

For the next hour or two Lisa helped Sarah pick out clothes to wear, but every time she needed to try on something she make sure her back was turned so no one who happened to be looking in their direction in the store would see her back. Lisa had the feeling that someone was watching them, of course she could have been paranoid since she knew Sarah's back held a secret so, Lisa kept Sarah as close to her as she dared when they left the store and headed back to base, they were carry three big bags of new clothes which also made her nervous because you can't control a blaster very well carrying stuff. But the once busy town was now almost empty since the last raid, most people were scared of another attack by the raiders when and if it comes again. It had been almost two weeks since the last attack and it was just by luck that they were beaten back and retreated. Many of the building had been destroyed or damaged in the attacks over the last six months and many people were fearful to the point that they couldn't even start rebuilding again. Everyone knew that they could not survive another attack, as they did not have the weapons to hold off another attack again.

Once they were back at the base Lisa took Sarah to the room that she had been assigned to stay while she was there and she helped put her new clothes in one of the dressers.

Sarah sat down on a chair in her room and watched Lisa put her new clothes away and looked around the room a bit.

After Lisa finished she walked over to Sarah, "Would you like to get something to eat? I know of a nice place to eat, John is going to be kind of busy

talking to his dad and uncles for a while I think, I know I'm hungry."

Jack left the meeting with John and his brother's, he needed to take a break and think about everything that had happened today. Walking into his office he felt the cold drift and dropped to one knee and bowed his head, "What is it my Mistress?"

Off to his right side heard a female voice, *"You must protect the girl at all costs, the raiders must not have her."*

From the left side he heard another female voice, *"There are many looking for her and what she carries, even thou she does not know what it is."*

Again from the right, *"Her life is in your family's hand, as you saved us so many years ago, we are entrusting her with you and your family. Your family must be careful because one of our sister has going mad with revenge and is helping the raiders!"*

Jack was not sure what to say next, "Can I ask what it is that she is carrying?" Feeling the chill leave the room he waited a few seconds and then stood up and looked around the room, and not seeing anything he went and sat down at his deck and started thinking about what he has just heard. This is the first time he had heard two of the Black Ghosts at the same time and that scared him a bit and he wondered what the girl was carrying that was so important to the Black Ghosts.

Peter Brown is storming around his office filled with rage as he listened to his friend Paul talking about the last raid and what had happened. "What do you

mean John escaped and many have the girl with him that I told you to get for me?"

Paul was trying not to look at his boss directly because he has seen what happened to those who made him angry and he was not ready to die today. "Somehow John got out of his jail cell and got to his ship, before we could find the girl. We do not even know how he found out about the girl, or if the girl is with him for sure, he had no way of even knowing we were after her."

Feeling a chill enter the room Paul took a deep breath as he ran his finger over the scar on the right side of his face, "We did not see where John had hidden his ship until it was to late to catch him. His ship was faster than any of those we sent to find the girl for you!"

Peter just stared at Paul as he tried to calm himself down, he has worked so hard to get where he is today as the leader of the raiders and he needed some time to think. "Get out and get as many ships together as you can to attack John's home world again!"

Paul turned and left the room as fast as he could and once out of the room, shook his head a few times. He was deep in thought about Peter; he was starting to go mad looking for all of that gold.

Once Paul is out of the room Peter turned and looked to his left and saw the thin outline of a female Black Ghost. "How did this happen? You said the girl was there and it would be easy to find her?"

The Black Ghost took a step closer and in an almost laughing voice, *"Your men were not fast enough. I told you were she was and how to find her. One of my good sister must have warned her and helped your friend to get away, but she does not know how important she is to you."*

Peter took one step toward the Black Ghost and raised his right hand and pointed his index finger at her, "We had a deal, you help me to get the gold and gems and I will take care of your sisters for you!"

The Black ghost took a step back, *"I told you the girl knew were the gold and gems are but she may not know anything at all. Find her and you find the gold and other things that will make you very rich far more then you could ever believe."*

Giving her a little laugh, "You talk in riddles, maybe you should just tell me where your sister are hiding so I can take care of them once and for all then look for the gold!"

She responded with sickening disdain, *"If only it was that easy to do as after the last person who try to get rid of them and failed found out, you can never find more than one at the same place or at the same time. But they all know that this girl needs to be protect for what she knows, so they may be close to her!"*

Peter looked toward a map of all the planets in the system and then back at the Black Ghost, "Look I need that gold to be able to pay my men, or I will loss them and everything we have been working for!"

Again the Black Ghost responded with evil in her voice, *"Just have them raid another girl's school. They like those young rich girls and they can keep some of them for a few days like they did on the last raid until their families have paid up!"*

Peter tried to give her a stern look but knew he was no match for any Black Ghost, "I do not need a lot of rich families looking for their young girls and finding them died or turned into sex slaves!"

Her manner then came to laughter, *"Then it would be best that you find that girl before your men leave you for something better!"*

Before he can say anything else she disappeared and they room suddenly grew warmer as he started to pace back and forth thinking and planning his next move. He then violently hit the communication board, "James I want your sorry ass into my office NOW!"

James walked over to his communication board and answered it, "Be right there boss." He then picked up his clothes and dressed hastily. He gave the young girl who is tried to the bed battered and nude a sick smile, "I will be back shortly my little one, so don't go anywhere. If you're rich daddy doesn't pay me soon I may send you to one of my entertaining house for my friends, they like 'em young."

Becky just stared at James with her only good eye left, after the beatings she received. After he left the room, she climbed off of the bed with her left hand still tied to the bedpost. She then reached under it and grabbed the loose spring from the mattress that she had found some time before and started working to free it again. For the last two days she had been working on the spring when that bastard left her lone. After about ten minutes the spring broke off of the bed it is about four inches long and she just stared at it. She knew that the next time he came back she would have to kill him, even though she cannot escape from this place. Death was better then this hell she was living in now. She slowly started to use the small piece of broken spring on the ropes around her wrist; she would rather die escaping then let anyone else touch her again.

James entered Peter's office and saw was Peter studying a map of the system with a sickening smile on his face. He looked up at James as he entered, "I want

you to take as many ships as you need and blockade the Planet Ares I have Paul getting the ships refueled ready for you."

Walking up to the table James frowned he was thinking about Becky and the other young girls he had locked up. He then looked down at the map to study it and then up at Peter, "There is nothing of value on Ares it's just a farming planet."

Peter took a step closer to James, his eyes wide with excitement "You have no idea what is on Ares! What is on Ares is worth over ten million credits to whomever can find it first."

Peter crossed his arm in front of him, James just looked back at the map and then at Peter, "Give me a clue, what we will be looking for, boss?"

"Not what, but who, is what you will be looking for." Peter answers beaming ear to ear.

With a big grin James started to plan his double cross to get the money or what ever it is, "Who will I be looking for?"

Peter walked over to a window and stared out, "The little girl that my old friend John Smith escaped with a few days ago while you were attacking that all girls' school, she is the key to a the credits and other things I want and need." He turned around and stared at James with chilling eyes, "Take ten ships and one refuel ship and blockade his planet until they give us what I want. It should not take too long because they are a farming planet and need to sell their crops in trade for what they need to live on."

James did not like the look in Peter eyes so he just nodded his head yes and he knew it would only take less then four ships to blockade the planet and one would be his large ship. His large ship is big enough for him to take at least three of his slave girls with to

help him pass the time with. But witch three of the six should he take with him is the question, and with any luck it will take at least a week to find and capture the girl if not longer.

Peter gave him a little chuckle because he knew what James was thinking, "Take only your smallest and fastest ships, I do not want them to get away with the girl this time, or you will not like what will happen to you and I promise it will be very painful!"

James swallowed hard he does not like pain and all thoughts of taking his big ship disappeared from his mind fast. He had seen what happened to those that got in Peter way. The look on some of there face was enough to make him change his mind.

Once out of the office he started to wonder what he could do to make this girl talk and tell him what Peter wanted to know. He wanted to use it himself to make himself rich. Walking down the hallway he spotted one of his men leaving a room that he know that another girl was being held for some of his fantasies and wild pleasures. He tried not to laugh when he saw that Hank had two fresh scratches running down the left side of his face and he was belting his pants.

Hank at first did not see James he was thinking about how fast that girl could move and her sharp nails, but she was not going to hurt him again if she lived that is.

James gave Hank a big smile. Hank was a very large man and a little over weight for James standard, but he love to hurt people with his fist and that believe it or not was an asset that was necessary, so his weight as overlooked. The only thing that Hank did not like to do was fly his ship in a fight, because of his size he hardly fit into his cockpit of his ship, and it was uncomfortable.

James reached into his pocket and took out a ring of keys as he neared Hank, "Hank I want you to look after my girls for a few days for me, I have to go away for a few days. I just want you to feed them and nothing ease or they will never find your body don't let anything happen to them!"

Hank took the keys out of James hand; "I got you covered boss as you can trust me to feed them for you." But Hank was Hank, and all he could think about was if James was gone for any length of time he would have access to a different variety and wondered how fun that would be, because he always had the pick of some very young pretty girls. It was not fair that James had the best looking girls from the all girl's school especially the fifteen year olds they took with them. James got to keep five of them and Hank got only two, which were the leftovers, and they were okay but not the best looking.

While Hank was daydreaming about his indiscretions, James began to see that Hank was not paying attention to him anymore and he just started at Hank for a few seconds almost as if he was listening to his thought, then he drew his knife and put it close to Hank's stomach, "If I find you out you do touch them in any way, you will die very slowly my dear good friend!"

A cold sweat started to run down Hank's back as he looked down at the knife at his stomach, he is not ready to die over some young girls, at least not yet. "You can trust me my good friend, I will just feed them and make sure no one comes near them."

James slowly pulled the knife away from Hank's stomach and put it back in sheath on his waist. "That had better be all that happens!" He then turned and headed back down the hallway. James already had

made a plan on how to blockade Ares and get that girl. Just maybe he could make her tell him where the gold was before he handed her over to Peter and get a head start going for it himself. There was nothing wrong with a little double cross once in a while, and it was for the moment just a thought in his mind, he just couldn't' get caught thinking it that is.

For the next two hours he gathered together the men he most trusted to follow him and what they are told without reservations or questions and will not report back to Peter about what he is up too.

Lisa walked into father's office with a sheet of paper in her right hand, on it was a drawn picture, and it was what she had seen on Sarah's back. She looked unhappy and depressed, "Father I would like to show you what is on Sarah's back, I saw it when we were shopping earlier today, and it is a tattoo of some sort of map I think. I drew a picture of it so I could show it to you and see what you think of it?"

Frank reached out and took the drawing from Lisa's hand and looked at it and then he looked back up at Lisa. He then took a magnifying glass out of one of the drawers of his desk. He studied the drawing over slowly. "It is a map, but I don't know to where? Who put this a map on Sarah's back?"

Lisa took a deep breath before explaining, "She said her mother and father did just before she was sold to her Mistress."

Before he could ask Lisa another question, they both heard the planets security alarms go off. Both of them run over to one of the windows and saw two raider ships flying close to the ground but not firing upon anything yet. While they both watched the raiders ships flying around they hear a noise behind

them and turned around and saw Tom entering Frank's office.

Tom was standing in the doorway he had a troubled look on his face, "They contacted me and told me that they want Sarah! If we do not turn her over to them, they are going to blockade our planet, until we do!"

Frank looked at him for a moment, then back at Lisa. Then he angrily shouted at Tom, "Find, John now! Lisa, you had better bring Sarah back here too, we need to have a conversation."

I was just finishing washing myself up and getting ready to have dinner with the Kirby twins; it had been a while since I'd seen them and we were about to meet in an hour. I planned on asking them to marry me, but suddenly heard a commotion outside and heard someone loudly banging on my bedroom door hard.

I looked at the door knowing that all this ruckus could not be good. "Enter, it's not locked."

Tom burst into the room his face, well I can't even describe that look… but he looked like a wild animal or a mad man, "You brought us some immense trouble this time and your dad is NOT very happy!"

I held out my hands and shrugged my shoulders, I wasn't trying to be disrespectful, "What and the hell are you talking about?"

He pointed towards the doorway his face was red with anger, "It's that girl you brought here, the raiders want her and they will not leave until they have her!"

I put one hand on my side and just stared at my uncle for a second, I wanted to give him a little breathing room to calm down before I spoke again, beside I had never seen my uncle this shade before, "Why would the raiders want her, she is just a slave

girl? And it was not my idea to bring her anyway, she just happened to find her way onto my ship with the help of her Black Ghost, so don't put this shit on me!"

Tom just walked up to me and shoved me toward the doorway hard, I began to turn around and give him all I had, figured I didn't want to hurt the old man and besides I was just curious. "It does not matter just move, now!"

All that was wondering through my mind is that Sarah was starting to be more trouble then she was worth, and that was not much, I also had a feeling that I was going to miss my dinner date with the twins.

All the way to my father's office I could hear ships flying overhead it was eerie in a way, that they were not firing at all, and I was wondered why the girl was so important to them, and if so was she important to us?

Once we entered my father's office that first thing I noticed was my father and a few others were all standing over a table examining a drawing and talking softly. Off to one side of the room on a sofa were Lisa and Sarah sitting together, they looked as baffled as the rest of us. Sarah looked a little bit scared because she knew this was all about her for some reason, so she was holding Lisa's hand in a pretty tight grip or is it seemed.

I walked straight up to the table ready for whatever was coming and took a deep breath, now I knew for sure that I was going to miss his dinner date with the Kirby twins, this could take hours, so I backed up a bit went over to my father's desk and made that dreadful call, then I rejoined the group around the table. I got in-between my father and my uncle Jack, I really wanted to stay as far away from Uncle Tom as I could

within reason, then I looked down at the drawing on the table that they were studying so intensely. "What is this?"

My father Frank never stopped to look at me when he answered, he was still looking down at the drawing, "It's on Sarah's back and what we think the raiders want!"

I did a quick glance over at Sarah and then back at the drawing, then I too started to talk softly "What do you mean on Sarah's back? What is it a drawing of? All I see is a drawing of different planets."

Uncle Jack leaned over the table and pointed at some of the symbols on the drawing, "These symbols mean gold and these mean some kind of gems I think."

I again gave Sarah a quick glance, "Who put it on her back and why?"

My father gave me a strange look and he too took a glimpse Sarah's way, "Sarah said her mother and father tattooed it on just before she was sold to the Black Ghost."

I shook my head in disbelief, "Tattooed, what parent would do that? Just give them the drawing and tell them it is what they want. Maybe they will leave us alone and leave her alone too."

I took a moment and looked at the girl, suddenly I was feeling a little guilt and concern for her, I never expected that to happen then I returned to looking at the drawing again. "We already tried that, but they want the girl and all drawing as well, in other words they don't want anyone else to have any information."

Standing by the window watching the raiders flying around was Adam, he turned my way, "I have talked to the farmers alliance and they do not want the girl hurt either, but they do need to be able to sell their crops soon, before they go bad and lose everything this year.

So may I suggest we work on this problem we do have a little time, but not much."

Lisa almost jumped off of the sofa, "I hope you are not even thinking about giving her to those animals! If she is lucky they will just kill her after they get what they want and once are done with her and that is the kind thing they could do! Otherwise she will be tied up beaten and raped until she either is of no use to them or dies!"

Frank took one step toward Lisa with his hands out in front of him trying to calm her down, "That is one thing we would never do, we do not want any harm to come to her as well, and if she is that important, there is a reason why"

Just then a man with a scar running down the left side of his face entered the room, "Sir, I do not mean to eavesdrop but those ship cannot fight this close to the planet only in the upper atmosphere, they don't have the capability they are long range fighters. They are probably just here as a scare tactic." He then approached me holding out his hand as a kind gesture, so I shook his hand, "My name is David Small and I used to work on the raiders ships until I saw what they were doing to people, especially the young girls in their possession." Pointing at his scare, "The boss Peter gave this to me when I told him I was leaving them and, I brought all of my men and their families with me here, and we have appreciated the way your planet treats people. I for one did not like the way some of the raiders were treating us who were loyal, some of them were even looking at my little girl, I felt like they were just biding time until she was old enough, they are animals, she (pointing over to Lisa) was correct!"

David walked over to the window and looked out at the Raiders as one flew by, "At the rate they are

burning a lot of fuel and they will have to go somewhere and refuel in a few hours unless they brought a large ship to refuel them, which of course again they would have to be higher in the atmosphere to do that."

I wasted no time making friends with this guy, I mean he was an ally to have, so I walked up to the window too, "I'm John, Peter used to be a friend of mine or so I thought at the time. I respect you and any information you can give to us about the Raiders, How many ships can they refuel at one time on one of those larger refuel ships, and how long will it take?"

David beamed with not only confidence but also pride; finally he had found a home and didn't have to hide who he had been associated with in the past, because to these people everyone matters. He turned toward me, "Three at time if they do not run into a trouble while refueling and it takes about ten minutes to refuel each ship."

My father walked up behind me and put his right hand on John's shoulder, "What are you thinking? If I may ask?"

I then turned around and walked back to the table with my new friend David and looked down at the drawing, "First we need to know where this map starts, you know like a reference point so we can beat the raider to whatever they are looking for, and I think it's the gold and gems that have been missing for a very long time."

Sarah suddenly looked up at Lisa, "I know why they want me, I just remember something my mother told me after they put that tattoo on my back she said to me that somehow I would be able to know what it is and how to get there."

Lisa all but jumped up off of the couch and moved over the table hastily, she looked at the drawing for a

moment "The only way Sarah could see this drawing on her back would be to be looking at it in a mirror, it's backwards!"

Frank looked over at David and shouted, "Get me a mirror, fast!"

David ran out of the room to retrieve a couple of mirrors as my father turned and smiled at Sarah and then looked at me, "Son I hope you have a plan to get off of this planet and follow the map if you can, that is?"

I just nodded yes my father suddenly looked almost joyful, if that was possible, "We will send out two or three of our fastest ships and have then head off in different directions for a distraction just as some of the raiders are refueling, then we only have a few flying around here and hopefully they will go after those ships, at the same time we make our move on out of here."

My Uncle Tom just shook his head still looking at the drawing, "Before we start to make any plans, lets see where the map tells us to go first."

Frank took the drawing off the table and walked over to one of the walls by the couch near where Sarah was still sitting. She looked very confused as he tacked the drawing to the wall.

At that moment David came back into the room carrying a very large mirror "I hope you do not mind me taking this large one out of the bathroom." He walked over to where my father was and held the mirror up so Frank could look at the drawing in its refection.

While Frank was studying the refection, everyone but my uncle Jack moved so they too could see the refection in the mirror. Jack slowly moved closer to me

and Sarah who stood up next to him, he put his hand on Sarah shoulder gentry.

Frank turned and looked at me and Sarah, "One of these planets was the home world of the female Black Ghost's it was called Titan! Why would Sarah have a map to the Black Ghost's home world? Unless that is where the gold and gems are hidden?"

Tom gave everyone a little laugh, "Who would think to look there for the gold and gems, if there is any gold or gems to begin with?"

Lisa pointed at the refection, "If that is where the gold is, why did she also paint the other planets on Sarah's back, I mean if she just wanted her to go to that one planet the other ones especially the outer edges don't make sense?"

I looked at my father, I and he were kind of puzzled, "Well it could be to hide which one is the one it is at, or unless the gold is hidden on all of the planets to make it harder for someone to get all of it, that is what I would have done!"

Tom pointed to one of the planets, "This one is called Rhea and it's a ice planet and the one next to it is called Dione and it's a water planet, the other one is called Janus and no one has ever seen the surface of it because of all of the gaseous clouds around it. If there is gold on one of them, you have also think about all their moons too."

I took a few steps away from the rest of them, I was deep in thought and then turned back toward the rest of them, "If we do go after the gold and whatever else is there we need to make sure that the Raiders do not follow us. Before we head to Titan, we should maybe stop at one of the other planets alone the way that is not on the map and make it look like we are looking on

them first for the gold just in case someone is watching."

Sarah moved over next to me and gave me a weak smile, "Why not just tell the Raiders where the gold is and maybe they will leave me alone?"

Jack walked over to Sarah and put his hand on her shoulder, "I wish it were that easy. If the raiders were to get their hands on the gold even if it is on Titan, they would just use it to buy a bigger ship and take over more planets and then no one would be safe from them."

Lisa got between Jack and me; "Before we even think about going after the gold, you need to think about the Raiders that are here now!"

David approached me, "Let me have my men watch the Raiders and find out when they go to refuel, then we can find out how long it takes them to do so, you can take off to do what ever you want to do once we have that time estimated. I for one do not want the Raiders to get the gold, they are corrupt now and we do not need them to get worse then they are! I for one do not want them to take over this system or any other systems."

Peter was pacing around his office he did not like to be kept waiting and should have heard from Paul or James by now. He does not understand why they just did not give the girl up. After all, the farmer's needed to export their grains to make a living. The Smith's never did bring in much credit from finding and returning things to Ares. He suddenly stopped pacing and headed over to the window to look out over his kingdom at all of the people. They would do whatever

he told them to do and if they didn't they knew they would die. Again that feeing of the cold draft entered he room and he stood up but did not turn around to face it, "What is now?"

He then felt the cold getting a bit closer and a hand touched his right shoulder, *"It might be a good idea to go and make sure that your friend Paul or James do not double-cross you and keep the girl for themselves and the gold. You are the only one I trust to get her and make her show you where the gold and other gems are. If the Smith goes after the gold and gems it would be the end to everything you have started here, you cannot trust them to just hand you the girl. You should not trust anyone this close to taking over this system."*

He nodded his head in agreement, "You are right, Paul or James would double-cross me if they knew they could get way with all of the gold and gems for themselves. Both of them would stab each other in the back to get their hands on it. Like I have always said, if you want something done right the first time, you have to do it yourself the first time!" He then felt the hand leave his shoulder turned and headed towards the door just before leaving he turned his head slightly and looked over his right shoulder, "You coming?" Not waiting for a response he left his office without looking back.

Once in space Peter set course for Ares he had hoped that he was not too late from stopping Paul or James from double-crossing him. He didn't check his radar, and so far no one had dared to attack him on his home planet he had become too important for anyone to dare a feat such as that.

But if he had checked his radar he would have seen a large group of ships coming fro, around the moon heading toward his home planet. All the ships banners showed they were from planets that he had had his raid within the last few months. They were battleships loaded with soldiers who were infuriated at him and his men. Unlike Peter's ships these are heavily armed for a long battle in space and they were all ready to take on his ships anywhere, anytime, and any place, as far as Peter's squads only were equipped for this type of battle and they were dead raiders.

As the commander Admiral Janet Cook was seated in the captain's chair watching the main view screen. She pounded her right fist on the chair's armrest as she watched the planet growing larger as they approached. Behind her were her husband Ben and her brother Jimmy Brown who were both in full combat gear, ready for battle and with blood in their eyes. Janet and her husband had service their King for over twenty year before retire to their farm to raise their daughter Becky. It had taken all of the credit they had left over from there service to get her into that all girl school, then her was taken from them by the raiders, and who knows what torture she had to endure. They did not need much persuasion to go after the raiders. When they were asked to lead the attack on their home world they jumped at the opportunity.

Janet spotted a raider's ship leaving the planet and struck a button on her armrest, "Send one of our ships to follow that ship and find out where it's going? But do not attack it, I want all of the raiders, DEAD, so we need a lead!" She then turned and facing her husband and brother, "Go and get ready to launch your attack shuttles and bring me their leaders head! Kill the rest so they do not regroup and start over again!"

Jimmy nodded his head and turned to follow Ben off of the bridge. He too was upset with the raiders; his own wife had worked at the school and had been killed there defending the school and children she loved so much.

Janet pushed another button on the other armrest, "Launch all shuttles when ready." When two King's and one Queen's had come to their farm and told them about the schools plight and Becky being one of the girls taken by the raiders, all she could think about was getting her back. She did not care about any credits that they were willing to pay to go after them, all she wanted was some ships and men at her disposal, then maybe she had a chance to get her daughter back. The though of her only daughter in the hands of the raiders made her see blood red.

David and his men were on the rooftops of several of the building in the town and on top of some of the farmer's dwellings as well, they were watching the raiders and keeping track of the ships. David was on top of Frank's building wearing a headset and communicating with his men all over the planet on the other building and writing down everything they were reporting back to him.

Frank climbed up a ladder and joined him on the roof; he walked over to him with a slight frown, "What have you learn so far?"

David held up his hand and then turned and looked up at Frank with a large smile, "I just heard that someone is attacking the raiders home world and Peter Brown has joined the raiders here." He then took the headset off, "There are ten raider that we have been able to track but only five at one time and the other five

or refueling. If you were to time leaving here and wait until the five are heading back up to refuel, you can get a little bit of a head start taking off and do what you need to."

Frank took one quick look back up at the sky and then toward David, "Try to give us heads up hour lead way before we can take off, it's going to take us a little bit to get ready to leave here." Without waiting for a reply he turned and walked back to the ladder and climb back down off of the roof.

Peter viciously slammed Paul up against the bulkhead, "NO, we are not heading home to save your precious slaves girls! Once we have the girl that we want, you can buy hundreds like them, so forget about them!"

Paul pushed Peter way from him as he just stared at him with bewilderment, "You had better be right about that girl. I do not care how many men I have to go though you will be a dead man!" He bumping Peter's right shoulder as he walked away from him and tried to calm himself down as he walked away.

Peter watched Paul walking away and thought about when this is over, when his time was done. He thought about just opening an airlock standing next to it because he had just about worn out his welcome.

Feeling the cold draft surround him there was a whisper into his left ear, *"He might be trouble and if you like I could take care of it for you later?"*

He did not dare to look at her but as he headed toward the bridge he answered, "Yes, once I have the gold and gems I will not need him and a few others I think." Peter hated being on refuel ships they were so

small and everyone had to share a room with at least three other men, at least when they were on a raid they were in shifts and he could stretch out a bit. He walked onto the bridge and pushed the captain of the chair and took a seat in it himself. "Any word from those thieves on when they will hand over that damn girl to us?"

Sam, who was his radio operator, shook his head and responded, "Not a word after they asked if the drawing was good enough?"

Peter slammed his fist down onto the armrest, "Tell the next group of ships heading down to blast where the farmers store their grains and then let's see how fast they listen to us this time!"

Before Sam gave the order to the ships heading down to the planet, another man on the bridge looked up from the radar, "Sir, there is a large long range ship leaving the planet at a high rate of speed!"

Peter leaned back in his chair with a crooked smile, "Recall all of the ships and follow that long range ship, but not too close, let's see where they are headed."

Sam looked at his leader and cautiously said to him, "Sir, it going to take about five minute to get all the ships back on board."

Slamming both fists onto his armrest, "Tell them to hurry back and do not loss that ship or I will have you all skinned alive if it they away from us!" He then got out of the captain's chair and started to pace around it as he was cursing under his breath about how long it will take to get all the ships back on board. Finally they all are aboard came over the speakers and he all but jumped back into the captain chair and shouted, "Follow that ship, but remember not too close, I do not want them to know we are following them."

I was sitting next to my father who was piloting one of his own ships; it was the biggest ship my family had. My uncles my sister and even Sarah had come on this trip. Sarah wanted to find out why her parents put that tattoo on her back and I didn't blame her, she also wanted to find out if the gold and gems were there too. I just wish I had more time to spend at home before we left, but the farmer were getting worried that they would not be able to ship their crops off and trade there goods. The twins were not happy that he was leaving so soon after just getting back and both started to cry when he told them I was leaving again.

Once we were in space everyone met on the bridge at a little table near the back usually used for mapping, we had to go over what planet we were going to look at first, and strategize in case we were followed.

I tapped one of the drawings with my index finger, "I say we checkout Rhea first then Janus and Dione and finely Titan."

My uncle Jack shook his head no, "I have to disagree with you I think we should head straight for Titan and get this over with as fast as we can! I hate playing games and want this over with. Besides I have a date waiting back home too."

Tom looked at Jack and then me he had his hands clasped behind his back, "We just cannot lead the Raider to where we think all of the gold is and we cannot fight them, so we need to at least visit one of the other planets first."

David walked up to the table from one of the consoles and addressed all of us, "Just like we thought, the raiders are following us but they are staying way back, hoping that we do not see them. I think they are

waiting to see where we are going before they make their move on us."

Frank looked around the table and with a scowl pointed at Titan, "It's my ship and we are going to Titan first and let the raider be damned, I never did like running from a fight in the first place!"

Lisa had been quietly listening she had been standing behind Frank with Sarah at her side she suddenly reached out and pulled Frank around so he was facing her grabbing his hand, "Just what are we going to fight them with, you have to think about the rest of us too this is not a game you are playing!"

Frank pulled his hand away from Lisa hard, "You just keep an eye on Sarah and leave the fighting to us! We have a few surprises for them if they want to fight us right David?"

David just gave Lisa a big smile, "This ship can fight in space unlike the raider ships."

Lisa took a few steps away from the men at the table with Sarah still at her side she was not happy, she only hoped that they knew what they are doing.

I moved a bit closer to Lisa, "I care for Sarah as well and don't want to see any harm come to her, but I want answer too. Who told her parents to put that tattoo on her back and why did the Black Ghost want me to take her with me when I escape from my jail cell?"

Tom looked down at the drawing, "It's going to take us two days to get to Titan at our top speed and we will pass Janus on the way. It might be a good idea to make it look like we are landing there; we could at least fly into the clouds down by the atmosphere for a bit. If we were to enter on one side and leave out the other side, it might buy us some more time on Titan. We may need it to find what we are looking for without being bothered

by the raiders. Titan is large and most of its building have been destroyed by King Artie."

My father Frank walked over between Lisa and me and looked at everyone, "Let us all take a step back it is going to take us while to get to Titan. We have lots of time to think about what we are going to do and when we are going to do it." He then slowly looked around the bridge, "It has been a long day for all of us so let us all turn in and we will sleep in shift, just in case the raiders try something before we get to where we are going."

I moved toward the captain's chair, "I'll take the first watch if no one ease want it?" Besides that's where I felt most comfortable.

My father looked at me before starting to head off the bridge, "I'll take the next one, wake me in four hours." Seeing me sitting in the captain's chair not only made my father proud but also reminded him of the years of training and time we had spent together when I was younger. He had a sort of grin on his face when he left the bridge.

Sarah started to leave the bridge with Lisa but stopped and walked over to me and put her hand on my hand, "I hope this works out and we all will get the answers we are looking for, John?"

I reached over and pat Sarah's hand, "Can I ask what you are looking for?"

Sarah looked out at the stars on the screen and then back at me, "Who I am?" She turned around and walked back over to Lisa they both leave the bridge and headed to the their quarters.

Once in her quarters, Lisa helped Sarah get ready for bed and then left the room to head to her own quarters. Once the lights were off, Sarah just lay there looking up at the ceiling, she felt the familiar cold draft

around her and it felt like someone something was pulling the covers up a bit, she was being tucked in like when she was a child and then felt a kiss on her forehead. Her eyes got large and she tears up a bit, the only other person who had ever tucked her in bed and kissed her like that, that was her mother!

Becky was not sure what was going on, the building was shaking and smoke was starting to fill her room. She heard loud explosion and a lot of shouting going on, someone was really angry and the voices just kept getting louder.

Becky got off the bed, she kept the wire at her had pulled off of the mattress at her side and slowly walked toward the door, not sure what to do, should she run? The room shook some more. Her mom and dad had always told her that as long as you can move you can fight back.

Hank was slowly moving down the hallway holding his bleeding right arm, he used his left hand tried to take the keys out of his pocket. He was not sure who was attacking them, but knew that he needed to escape somehow, he needed a hostage to help him get to his ship and he knew just whom it would be. He may or may not let her go once he escaped, he liked them young and she was young and rich, or so he had be told. He was fumbling with the keys and once he got them out of his pocket, it took him a few seconds to find the right key for the door, with bloody fingers he put the key into the lock and opened the door.

Becky had moved so she was standing right in front of the door with the wire in her hand, she knew that she will go down fighting who ever opened the door.

Hank opened the door and took one step into the cell he just stood there in shock to see that the young girl was standing in front of him just staring at him with a look of pure hated in her eyes. Before he can take another step toward her, she moved swiftly toward him with her hand out and as soon as she could, she leapt forward and he felt something hit his neck. He reached up and was surprised to find that there was blood coming out of his neck, then some started to come out of the corner of his mouth. He took one step back toward the hallway as he tried to pull whatever it was out of his neck, but before he could pull it out he was hit in the side the head by a blaster and fell to the floor dead his head had a gaping wound.

Becky just started at him and before she could move a man dressed in full battle gear stepped in front of the doorway.

Jimmy raised his helmet visors and had a horrified look on his face at the sight of his naked, battered niece in front of him, "BECKY we are here to get you out and take you back home!" She stepping over Hank's dead body and Jimmy took off his battle jacket and put it around her, the exhaustion, fear and thought of being free finally overwhelmed and she looked like she was about to pass out in her uncle arms. He picked up Becky and her body went limp, he carried her into the hallway. Some of his other men were also carrying other girls out of their cells. As he was carrying Becky out of building he has to cross over some of the dead raiders who had tried to stop them from entering the building, he just held Becky close to him so she would not have to see the carnage. Many of the building around them were starting to catch fire from the fighting or have been set on fire by the attacking forces.

Near one of the shuttles he saw, Ben standing by directing the rescue mission, and when Ben saw Jimmy carrying his daughter he stepped forward with his hands out, "I'll take her, you go back and make sure we do not leave any of the girls behind!" He took Becky into his arms and then turned and headed into the shuttle shouting as was entering it, "I need a doctor, STAT!"

Jimmy ran back into the building looking for some other girl to carry out, but all he saw was that all the cells were now empty. He saw some of his men dragging a man down the hallway, the man looked like he has been beaten pretty bad and was begging for his life? Jimmy pulled out his blaster, walked up to the man and put the barrel right in his mouth and sneered, "Where is your leader?"

The man was shaky and his voice cracked, *"He want to Ares to find a girl who knows where there is a lot of gold and gems are hidden!"*

Then he looked up at the men who were surrounding the man, "The Admiral said no prisoner." He squeezed the trigger, not even looking down at the man on the floor whose eyes had the look of terror just before he shot. "Back to the shuttles once we have all the girls safely on board. So check ever room in this building really good, as we are not leaving any of them behind. Then burn this place down we do not want any more raiders to use is place again!" He was trying to stay calm as he walked though the building checking every room and closet for anyone that might be hiding or in case some girls were still locked up somewhere. Finely he heard over his headset that all the girls were on the shuttle, so he headed out of the building as his men started setting some fires, as he was going to the shuttle he was beyond caring about what happened to

the town near the raider's main building. The town had lived off of the profits of the raiders for too long, now they were going to pay for that mistake.

Once outside of the building he walked straight toward the shuttles, never looking back at the building that was now fully engulfed in fire as well as some of the other building surrounding it.

Ben watched as Jimmy was coming toward him and the look on his face was anger and disgust Ben also watched the raider's building aflame.

Jimmy walked right up to Ben, "Their leader is heading toward Ares on that ship that left just before we attacked here."

He turned toward the other men, Ben waved and shouted, "Load back up then head back to the mother ships, and our work here is done!" He then turned and walked back into the shuttle and over to the bed his daughter was resting on as a doctor was working on her cleaning face with a wet cloth.

The doctor saw both Ben and Jimmy heading toward Becky he felt the ship take off and waved them over to the side he had a worried look, he put his hand on Ben's shoulder, "She has been raped a few times all the girls have been that I have check so far. The physical injures will heal; it's the ones we cannot see that will take time! I promise you that when we get them all back home, they all will get the best care their Sir."

Ben just looked at his daughter with a look of sadness in his eyes and then looked at Jimmy, "I want you to go with them once we get abound our main ship, and I want all of the girls sent to their home world as soon as possible for treatment."

Jimmy gave Ben a stone cold look, "SIR, I want to make their leader pay for what he did to my wife at the

school and all of these girls not just Becky, SIR!" As he stated that he was waving his hand around motioning to all of the girls and a tear fell from his eye.

Ben put his right hand on Jimmy's shoulder, "I know you want ravage, but your wife would also want you to look after her girls for her."

Just then they felt the shuttle land and within a few second the door opened and the Admiral all but ran into the shuttle and after a quick look around, ran over to her daughter and wrapped her arms around her. She gave her daughter a kiss on the forehead and then turned and walked over to Jimmy and Ben with a stern look on her face, "Tell me you got their leader?"

Ben shook his head, "No he is on his way to Ares he heard that some girl there knows where a lots of gold and gems are hidden."

The Admiral looked over at Becky once more and then back at Ben, "That is where the ship is heading that just left here just before we attacked. I want their leader and I want him alive I have something special planned for him!"

Ben reached out and took the Admiral by the elbow and led her away from Becky, "We are sending all of the girls to their home worlds and then we will go after their leader and the rest of the raiders."

The admiral nodded her head in agreement then turned and walked back to Becky and gave her another hug and then walked out of the shuttle with an intense look on her face.

James walked onto the bridge and the first thing he saw is both Peter and Paul looking over some space chart. All James could see was Peter's back and how

good it would feel to stab him with a knife in it at the moment. Too bad no one was allowed to carry any weapon on this ship. He tried to compose himself and took a deep breath before he approached them and when he did he saw about four planets on the chart they are looking at.

Peter turned and gave James a scowl, "Its about time you decide to join us! As far as we can tell, there are four planets they could be heading to, Janus, Dione, Rhea or Titan."

James just returned his stare; "I want to make sure all of our ships are refueled, just in case we need to send all of them out in a hurry!"

James pointed at one of the planets; "If I was to hide something I did not want found, I would hide it on Janus, with the all of those clouds it would make it hard to find anything down on it."

Paul pointed at Dione, "I would use Dione all I would have to do is drop the package and come back later when I was ready to collect it." Pointing at Rhea, "Rhea would be too hard to hide anything on, with all of the ice you would have to dig to hide anything and it would take a while."

James looked at all of them he was puzzled "What about Titan? With all those burned out building, it would be a perfect place to hide stuff and no one would think of looking there. Some even say it is haunted by all the dead female ghost, who use to live there."

Peter tapped the map on the planet Titan, "I'm willing to bet that is where they are heading, so let's let them go to the other planets first and try to miss lead us, while we go and get the stuff!"

James sternly looked at Peter, "What if you're wrong?"

Peter just stood up straightened his jacket then he gave them a broad smile, "You will just have to trust me on this, they all looked back down at the other planets on the map then he made a statement that all of us were eager to hear we will get rich beyond our dreams." He then turned and walked off of the bridge with a sinister laugher.

James looked at Paul with a revolting smile, "Someday he will have a little accident with my knife!"

Paul grabbed James arm and leaned in close, *"Keep your voice down he has spies everywhere."*

I was looking at the radar as we were nearing Rhea, I spotted a ship following us and heading straight for Titan. I looked up from the radar at my father, "The raiders are heading straight for Titan for some reason?"

My father Frank got up from the captain's chair and moved over to the radar to get a look himself, "This is not good, either they know something we do not know or they are guessing where the gold is and want to get there before we do!" He then took a step back and put his hands on his hips, "This changes everything, we need to get everyone together and decide our next move."

Uncle Jack was in his cabin down on one knee his head down as he felt the chill in the air again, "My mistress, are we doing the right think?"

From his left side he heard a whisper, *"You need to go right to Titan time is very essence as if the raider get*

there first, it could mean trouble for everyone in this system and beyond it!"

From his right side he heard the other ghost's, voice *"You must be on the lookout for one of our sister's who has gone mad all she dreams about is power and she will destroy those of us who are left! We are the only ones who know how to stop her for good so be careful around her, she loves to hurt people and is manipulative."*

Jack heard the call throughout the ship that everyone was being called back to the bridge so he got up and heading out of his cabin wondering how he was going to get Frank and the rest of them to go to Titan first. Once on the bridge he saw everyone looking down at the radar screen and Frank was not happy at what he was seeing on it.

Frank looked up from the radar, "The raider are heading straight for Titan. It looks like they may know more then we do or have guess at where we are heading."

I was still staring down at the radar, "I just noticed that there may be another ship following the raiders. It is traveling so far behind them that the raiders may not even know it's there? But I saw it, I think our radar is far more advanced then theirs, at least I was hoping so."

David walked over and looked down at the radar and then looked over at Frank, "If the raiders find the gold first and get away, it will mean trouble for everyone in this system and even beyond. We also need to find out who is following them and why. It may be more raiders or someone hunting them which could become our greatest ally in this conflict."

I agreed with his thinking, and couldn't keep myself from starting to pace around the bridge, "This is not

good, if it more raiders it will make our job just that more difficult to handle and if its someone hunting them? They may not care if we are friends or foe? I mean we could just be in the way of their goal, or they could get behind us and help us deal with them, either way we should figure this out and quickly."

Lisa and Sarah entered the area of the bridge together and Lisa looked around at everyone with a look of concern look on her face, that girls had a gift for reading people, "What is going on know?"

I just walked over to her and put my hand on her shoulder, "It's the raiders at the moment they are not following us which could mean they know something we don't, and someone is also following the raiders and we don't know what their intentions are. The raiders are heading straight to Titan and we are not sure what to do next but a whole entire shit storm could follow."

Lisa glanced over at Sarah and then looked back up at me, "We need to find that gold first, you know what would follow if we don't, that is all I know!"

I looked over at my father and then at my uncle sometimes was off but I couldn't yet put my finger on it, "What do we know about Titan?"

My father Frank pulled out a drawing of Titan and studied it for a moment or two then he pointed to a spot on it, "From what I have been told a female ghost build one small town right here on this small island. Most of the rest of the planet is water all but for this spot and this other large land mass, but that has nothing on it but a tall mountain that was a volcano a couple hundred years ago."

My uncle Jack looked down at the map of the planet and then looked up at Frank, "The volcano is over a hundred mile in diameter at it's base and that is where I would hide something I did not want someone

else to find because it would not be an easy task, and really dangerous I bet there are some caves there too."

I looked down at the map and then at the drawing that was made from the tattoo on Sarah back. I noticed something and pointed it out on the drawing, "Look, what is on the corner here of the drawing, does that not look like a volcano to you?"

Everyone moved over to the drawing and looked down at it closer. Jack took a step back, "The volcano is on the opposite side of the planet that is the small island the town is on."

My father grinned broadly at everyone, "Lets wait till the raiders have landed on the island and then we will head to the volcano and see if we can find any caves there."

Sarah slowly looked up at everyone, "What if there are no cave? Then what will we do?"

My father moved over to Sarah and puts his hands on her shoulders, "Then we will head to the town as fast as we can and hope they have not found the gold, by the time we get there. If they have found it, it will take time to retrieve it and we will have to find a way to take it away from them!" I kept thinking great we will probably need to battle the raiders and that was not really what I had hoped for. My father then addressed everyone, "Let's hope that other ship is not looking for us and is only following the raiders, perhaps it is a good omen."

David turned to leave the bridge; "I will get some gear ready that we may need if we find any caves to go into, and we should probably get everything battle ready in case we need to go after the raiders."

I on the other hand had some thinking to do I walked to the front of the bridge and looked out the view screen to gather my thoughts, "I have a bad

feeling about this, something tells me that the raiders may know more then we do or they thing they do."

My father walked up behind me, "They have no way of knowing what is on Sarah's back. I think they are just guessing what planet we are heading for, I am confident they do not know about the island with the volcano on it, or so I hope."

Lisa put her arm around Sarah, "If you want we can stay on the ship while they look around?"

Sarah just sadly looked over at Lisa; "I have the feeling I need to be there too, so let go with them into any caves that they may find there."

Lisa retrieved her arm from Sarah and nodded her head, "Okay, but stay close to me then, I can't let anything happen to you."

Frank had moved over to the radar and is viewing the planet and the raider's movements; "The raiders are now heading down to the town, so change course now and head towards the island with the volcano it."

Peter, James and Paul are standing on the bridge looking out the window at the planet Titan as it got closer and larger in front of them. Peter had a bit of a crooked smile on his face, he was planning in his head the accident that James and Paul would have once he has all of the gold and gems, he will no longer need them again!

When they are almost on the surface Peter turned and looked at them, "The gold must be in one of the bigger building that are still standing."

James leaned a bit forward, "King Artie, really did a number on this town from the looks of things, there does not look like there is any building still standing."

Paul rubbed his chin, "King Johnson and his wife may have buried it somewhere or hidden it in one of the collapsed buildings that is what I would have done."

Peter turned and headed off the bridge, "I want everyone out with picks and shovels looking, till we find the gold and gems!"

James just smiled, all he was thinking about was what Peter's head would look like with a pick in it or a shovel on the neck. "We got your cover boss."

Paul not saying anything he had too had his own plans for these two and the gold and it was not a nice picture. He knew that once the Smith saw that they were not being followed, they would head straight here. That is when he would make his move, when everyone was fighting the Smith's and he had hand pick the bridge crew.

Once on the ground everyone got off of the ship but the bridge crew, who had been ordered to keep an eye open for the Smith's. Everyone had a pick or a shovel and fanned out all over the ruined town to start looking for the gold with the dream of striking it rich. Each raider thinking the same thing, and that was they would be the only one to leave this planet alive with the gold and gems if there were any.

Peter knowing his men, didn't trust any of them so he never had his back turned to any of them, he pointed out some of the bigger burn out buildings. "Check those out first they do not look to bad."

James looked around and turned to some of the raiders, "Look for places that they could have buried the gold and be quick about it."

For the next hour everyone is looking in every building and digging in different spots looking for the gold.

Peter was getting madder by the minute he slowly walked into what looked like was a big hall of some kind at one time, ten chairs lined each side, with one big chair at the end of the hall. He looked around he just smiled to himself this must have been the meeting place for the Black Ghost before King Artie wiped them out or so he though. The only thing missing from this large hall was the roof and one wall. He suddenly felt the coldness of his Black Ghost, "Where is it, my friend?"

Feeling the cold draft moving closer. *"It is not here, it must be at the other hiding place!"*

Pulling out his blaster he turned around, "WHAT OTHER HINDING PLACES?" His blaster was at the ready but there was nothing to see.

From behind him he heard his Black Ghost, *"There is an island with a volcano on it on the other side of this planet, and it is a place that scares even me as it is where we all started out as Black Ghost! No one dared to enter."*

Feeling his anger growing inside of his head as he stormed out of the great hall and started to shout at all of the men. "Its not here! There must be somewhere else on this planet that it is hidden!" Not wanting to tell them, that he know of another island on this planet or how he found out about it, he waved all the men back on to the ship.

I piloted the ship around the volcano twice before we spotted what looked like a small cave near its southern base. I landed as close as I could to the

opening, with the side of the ship with the hatch facing the cave opening. Once everyone was on the surface, David took the lead with his weapon ready in case there was any trouble and he led the group into the cave opening. Once inside the cave all of our jaws dropped, first thing we saw was approximately twenty glass cylinders up against one wall and in the middle of the room was something that looked like a sarcophagus with a drawing and writing on it.

Lisa and Sarah were the last to enter the cave following the rest of the group, but when Sarah came upon the drawing on the sarcophagus, eyes lit up, "DAD!" She ran up to the sarcophagus and placed her hands on top of it and started to sob. She then turned around toward the rest of us looking startled like she just realized we were there, "Where is my mom?"

My father Frank walked over to the sarcophagus and looked at the drawing and the write and then looked back at the rest of us, "It's King Johnson!"

I was too busy looking around the room at all the glass cylinders with a puzzled me to say the least "What are those used for?"

Everyone but Lisa and Sarah walked over to the glass cylinders Lisa was staying as close to Sarah as humanly possible, Sarah still was sobbing, it was almost getting to me.

David moved up close to one of the cylinders and looked into it and then took a step back, "I have never seen anything like this before!"

I scouted the place out; taking a look around, I was extremely on edge something just spooked the hell out of me. "Lets find the gold and get the heck out of here I have a bad feeling about this place!"

Sarah started to look around the room, at least she had quit her annoying incisive whining, and she then looked down some other passageway for the gold.

Lisa blurted out as we started looking around, "You guys go ahead and look around, and I will stay here with Sarah."

Sarah then looked up at Lisa her were red eyes from crying, "Where is my mother, she should be here too you would think?" Her eyes slowly scanned the room and suddenly she felt cold draft enter the room.

Lisa also felt the cold draft and wrapped her arms around herself trying to stay warm, she wish she was anywhere else but here.

Sarah reached and grabbed Lisa by the elbow, "I think my mistress is here?"

Lisa put her hand on top of Sarah shoulder as she felt the room starting to get even colder then she lead Sarah toward one of the passageways the men had gone into, "Stay close to me."

Just as they are nearing one of the passageways, they heard us men coming back. We were pulling a very heavy cart. David and I were in front pulling on the tongue of the cart and my father Frank and Tom were pushing and uncle Jack was pulling a smaller one. I gave the girls a very large grin, "We found four carts just like this one down at the end of this passageway and look here some have gold bars and precious gem stones on them!"

Suddenly they hear from the entryway a loud voice, "I WANT TO THANK YOU FOR FINDING MY GOLD AND GEMS FOR ME!"

We all turned around and saw Peter in front of Paul and James and about five other men; they are all and are pointing their weapons at us.

Peter waved his men to moved out and surround everyone from behind then slowly he walked up to me, "I do not know how to say think you for finding my gold for me." He then looked around at everyone and backhanded me across the face he might of even left a mark, "If you had giving me the girl when I asked you to give her to me, it would have saved you a lot of pain." His eyes then glared over at Sarah, and he gave her an evil grin; "Maybe I just will take her with me so my night do not get cold." Then he gave a very sickening laugh as he waved his men to take possession of the carts. He then turned and walked over to Sarah and Lisa with an evil smile, "Maybe I will take both of you with us. I might even share you with my men, for a reward for a job well done!"

I just couldn't take any more of his bull, and took a few steps toward him, I needed to confront him "Hey, I've got a question for you, old friend? Why did you send me to return that necklace if you know I would end up arrested and put in the slammer?"

Peter just laugh at me then he pointed toward the scar on his face, "I wanted your girlfriends, but they would not have me and I when I told them you were not coming back for a long time, one of them pulled a knife and marked me for life! If their father had not walked in I would have killed them both for this!" So there was my answer, it had to always involve some chick.

Lisa started to raise her hand to slap him but a loud noise startled all of us, and we realized the cave entrance was secured by a steel door. Lisa took a step back and pulled Sarah behind her and while we were all distracted started to move toward the others and me. She didn't get very far, before she could get the both of them in a safer position Peter grabbed her by the elbow, "Not so fast my pretty ones." He looked over his

shoulder at Paul and James and his men, "Get that door open, so we can leave this place with our gold."

James, Paul and the his men run toward the closed opening, but all Paul could think of is all of that gold and how he would like to take that young girl, Sarah for himself. Once at the opening all the men started to look for a way to raise the door blocking the entry to the cave, but cannot find anything to open it, or anything to pry it open either. Two men pulled out their blasters and took a few shots at the steel door, but the shots do nothing to the steel. Both men turned and headed back toward Peter and the rest of the group. All of them felt the cave starting to get very cold.

Peter watched us, as me and Paul ran back toward him and he felt the cold chill in the air of his mistress or so he thought, but this time the cold was not the same as all of the other times she was near him. Before he could say a word, the air in the cave started to swill around everyone as it got colder and colder and suddenly he heard his mistress scream out, *"NO, LEAVE ME ALONE, HELP ME!"*

I was not sure what was going on at all, I mean this voice came out of nowhere; I wasn't even sure where the cold wind was coming from. With the entry to the cave blocked no one wanted to be left alone in any part of the cave. But then my uncle Jack walked up next to me and whispering, *"Do not ask any question, just do what I do and listen."* I watched as my uncle Jack got down on one knee and bowed his head with one arm out in front of him. I kind of freaked I was thinking what the heck was this all about, then I watched my father and my other uncle and even David got onto one knee. I was still hearing a female voice out of nowhere screaming in pain so I thought I might as well follow suit, I mean wheat have we got to lose at this point, so I

too got down onto one knee then the cave started to get real cold, you could see a our breath hang in the air.

Peter was looking around the cave as he heard his mistress screaming out in pain again and the wind picked up even more. "What is it? What is happing here?"

Suddenly the wind stopped and around the room are several Black Ghosts maybe twenty in all, and in front of them is Peter's Black Ghost on her hands and knees.

Peter just stared at all of the Black Ghosts terrified at what they may do to him or her then he looked at the one on the floor, she turned toward him and in a loud voice said, *"KILL THEM BEFORE THEY STOP YOU!"* One of the Black Ghosts took a step toward her and in an angry voice echoed, *"BE QUITE SISTER AS YOU HAVE BROKEN OUR CONVEN AND ABOUSED THE GIFTS THAT WERE GIVING UNTO YOU."* All at the same time the Black Ghosts raised their hands up to shoulder level and the Black Ghost on the floor started to rise and moved toward the cylinders. One of the cylinders started to open and as the Black Ghost near it and then she screamed out, *"NO, NOT THAT I WILL BE GOOD, I PROMISE, HELP ME PLEASE!"* She reached out toward Peter, *SAVE ME!"*

Peter tried to raise his weapon, but he hands could only watch in horror as she went into the cylinder. Once she was inside of the cylinder it started to fill with a white smoke she tried desperately to get out, finally we could not see her any more. A few minutes passed and the smoke cleared away and all that was left was an older woman on the bottom of the cylinder crying, her clothes were tattered and when the cylinder opened she looked up the other Ghost, "Please change me back I will be good this time."

The Black Ghosts turned and looked at my family and me and then approached us, they looked like they just glided over the stone surface, *"She can no longer hurt anyone she has been stripped of her powers for good! You can do want ever you want to do to her as we do care what happens to her as we cannot hurt one of our own. Take the gold and gems and leave this place and never come back here again because this place will not be here much longer."* She then turned and looked at Peter and his men, *"Leave this place at once or you will never leave it and take her with you."* Pointing at the older woman who was still in the open cylinder crying loudly.

Peter gave her a little laugh and then point at Lisa and Sarah, "I think I will take these two with me too." But he heard a thunderous roar of laughter coming from the Black Ghosts and one of them went toward him, *"If you even try to take these two females you and your men will not live to see the next day."*

Just then everyone heard the entry to the cave open slowly and to the shock of everyone who had been trapped inside was Admiral Janet Cook, her husband and about ten of her men standing there. Then they walked into the cave with the weapons drawn and pointed at the Raiders.

Admiral Cook was focused on only one thing and that was Peter. His men were standing in front of my family and me and the older woman was crawling out of one of the cylinder. I can't even imagine what was going though her mind with this scene. She walked up to Peter with a glare in her eyes that would make any man terrified, pulled out her knife and pointed it at his stomach, "You and your men are coming with us, you are under arrest for rape, kidnapping, murder and I

Will think of more you can be charge with for crimes against the planets in this system!"

My father Frank got up off of his knees and took a few steps toward the admiral and pointed at the older woman, "That woman was helping him in his crimes and needs to go with him and his men."

Peter looked around the room his eyes were open really wide and filled with wonder, "Where did the Black Ghost go? They were here just a minute ago!"

Admiral Cook looked around the empty cave, "What Black Ghosts? I do not see any Black Ghosts and from what I have heard throughout history is that they were destroyed many years ago by King Artie. My own father was with him when he killed them all!"

Peter now looked around the cave wildly and then he pointed at the older woman, "Ask her who she was, she was a Black Ghost just a short while ago!"

Admiral Cook raised her right and hand to about should height and with two fingers pointed at the older woman, two of the men with her and started to drag her out of the cave.

The older woman tried to stop them but couldn't, she didn't have the strength anymore all she could do was shout, "Please do not let them take me my sisters!"

One of then men looked at Admiral Cook who just nodded her head, he then hit the older woman on the side of her head with his blaster. Once she as knocked out, the men just drag her out of the cave without saying a word.

Peter watched the two men drag the older woman out of the cave and then looked at the Admiral, "Look let make a deal, there is more then enough gold for everyone here."

Without even taking a look at him, she swung the base of her knife and hit him on the temple and he

dropped to the ground, which was a pretty neat trick, "I do not make deals with murders and men who kidnap and rape young girls." She looked at James both James and Paul, "You both are going to pay for your crimes too, along with as all raiders the on your ship the ones outside keeping watch and those with you here."

Paul had a very sick feeling in the pit of his stomach as he watched Peter try to stand up after being knocked out, but his legs were just wobbly and just would not hold him. The Admiral just kicked him in the stomach and knocked him back down.

The admiral then gave all a little smile, "Get him up and carry him to my ship and be quick about it." She watched as Paul and James took ahold of Peter's arm and started to drag him out of the cave, two of her other men kelp a close eye on all of them. Once we were out of the cave she walked over to Lisa and Sarah and looked back at the sarcophagus she seemed somber, "He was a good man and I was proud to have service him once and I was very sad when I heard he was being over thrown. I tried to come to his aid, but I was too late and I never found out what happened to his wife or their newly born baby girl I never forgave myself."

Sarah looked up at the Admiral with a tear in her eye, "He was my father and I do not know what happen to my mother?"

The Admiral put her right hand on Sarah's shoulder and looked at Lisa along with the rest of us who were standing next to the cart. "The gold belongs to her. Will you be the ones responsible to raise her until she is old enough to take care of herself you have shown already that you are worthy since you have brought her this far?"

I walked up to the Admiral and looked her in the eye, "You have our word that she will be treat good well and she will get the gold and the gems."

The Admiral looked around the room at the men standing near the cart, "You better make sure she does or I will find you and you will not want me to, because I will m not be nice." Without another word she then turned and walked out of the cave with the rest of her men.

Lisa looked at me and then gave the cave a glance one more time, to her surprise the Black Ghosts were back again. One of the Black Ghosts took a few steps toward them and stopped right in front of Sarah. "*My daughter I'm so sorry, please forgive me. I made the mistake of falling in love with your father ad asked to leave the sisterhood of Ghost and marry him. But once they came to overthrow your father, the only way I could keep you safe and alive was to sell you to one of my sisters and be turned back into a ghost again. I tried to stay as close as I could because I wanted you to live."* She then guided over to the sarcophagus and put her right hand on it and bowed her head and everyone heard her start to cry softly. After a few minutes she turned around and looked at us still tearing up, "*The gold and gems belong to my daughter and she can do what she wants with it, once she is a bit older she can make her own plans. In the mean time I think you so very much that you will take care of her and the gold and gems for her."* Again she looked at her daughter, *"When the time is right and if you so wish it, you too can be one of us, but for now please live your life to the fullest, for it has only just begun."* With that all the Ghost disappeared but one of them and she guided up to Jack, "*Take the gold and gems and leave this place, and never come back, soon this place will not be here*

because the volcano is about to awake again from its slumber." **Then with that she just disappeared so did all od the cylinders and the sarcophagus, the ground started to shake a little bit which rattled all of us.**

My father Frank shouted, "Get everyone out of the ship to help us load the gold and gems before this volcano erupts!"

For the next hour everyone, including Lisa and Sarah helped load the gold and gems onto the ship and when we left the planet we saw the volcano start to smoke and then it erupted spewing its red-hot liquid down the mountain. I'll never forgot the picture in my head of Sarah's plea, just before we finished loading the last of the gold, Sarah had walked to the back of the cave and with one small box of gold and a small bag of gems, she got down onto her knee and bow her head and closed her eyes, "Is there any way you can send this to the planet where the school was destroyed and give it to them who are rebuilding it?" When she opened her eyes the box and gems were gone and Sarah just smiled to herself, "Thank you."

Once in space my dad and me walked to the back of the ship and saw Sarah and Lisa going though some of the gems and sharing a few laughs.

We pulled up two chairs and sat down, my father looked at all the boxes of gold and gave Sarah a little laugh, "So what are you going to do with all of your gold and gems if I may ask?"

Sarah just looked at the gems in her hands and then at the two of us, "I want to go to school and learn to help others who have nothing like I me before I came to meet your family." She give me a large smile, "I also want to share it with your family and the people of this system to do good things, they have lost so much from the raiders, and I especially want to help the poor."

My father looked at me and I knew the emotions were stirring inside, and then he looked back at Sarah, "I think we can set something up for everything that you wanted, and as for you going to school that is a very good idea. All kids should to go to school and soak up everything they can when they're young with all of this gold and gems you have it will be very important to learn as much as you can."

Admiral Cook was on the bridge looking out at the stars, her husband entered the bridge and stood next to her and just nodded his head yes. She then pushed a button on her armrest and you could see on the main view screen are seven people who appeared wearing space suits. One was Peter, his two highest-ranking men the ex Black Ghost and the rest of his Raiders. Peter looked at the Admiral with fear in his eyes and shouted, "You cannot do this, it's will be murder!"

The Admiral then give them all a stern look, "I'm thinking about all of those that you have killed in your raids, I want you to think about them and remember every face of the girls you have harmed as you run out of air!" She didn't wait for a reply, she just pushed another button and the cargo bay doors opened and they floated out into space. She then closed the doors and looked at her husband, "That should be a warning to all raiders I hope."

Ben Cook just looked out at the stars, "It also saved some of the Kings the cost of a lengthy trial."

Admiral Cook just looked out at the stars, "Let's go home we need to checkup on Becky and we have crops in the field that will need to be harvested soon."

Jimmy was busy looking at some blueprints on a table just outside of the buried out school, when one of his workers came running up to him, "Sir, we just found something you need to see."

Jimmy gave the worker a puzzle look and followed him into the school; right in the middle of the room was an open box with gold bars and some gems. On top of the gold bars was a note, Jimmy reached down and picked it up and read it, "Use this gold and gems to rebuild your school and also to allow the girls who cannot pay to go here too." Down on the bottom corner of the note was a black mark, which faded away when he read it. He turned and looked at the men around him with a smile, "We no longer have to worry about the cost of repairs or any girls having to pay to come here, at least for while."

One of the men, looked at him puzzle, "But where it come from? It was not here a minute ago!"

Jimmy looked down at the note again and then at the men around him, he folded the note and put it in his shirt pocket. "It does not matter where it came from, all that counts is that we put it to good use." He walked back outside of the school and back to his blueprints, he had heard stories of the Black Ghost, but had also heard that they had been wiped out a long time ago. Of course he never knew if any of the stories were true but now he knew for sure and also had heard about the Black Ghosts doing good things and assisted to stop wars. A new beginning, a fresh start was all that Jimmy had in his mind.

Just then King Blair was climbing down from the roof where he had been working all morning his wife Queen Sandy approached and got of a vehicle with

lunch for all of the workers. She still has big bandage on her arm from fighting the fire at the school.

Jimmy walked over to King Blair and took the paper out of his pocket and showed it to him, just as Queen Sandy walked up to them too.

King Blair read it and then showed it to his wife, "I think this is the work of your sisters."

Queen Sandy gave her husband a little shove, "Not so loud, they might hear you and they like to do things in secret, my love." She watched her husband climb back up the ladder to go back to work on the roof. Closing her eyes she looked at up at the sky, *"Thank you my sister, it will go to good use."*

Ten years later Sarah was saying her good byes to us, and then she turned and boarded her shuttle to leave us for good. I was holding one of my three babies; believe me when I tell you that I have been really busy, and that is an understatement "My wives will miss you being our nanny these last five years have been great having you around kid."

Sarah just smiled at me then Lisa approached carrying her own baby boy in her arms, "I will come back someday to check on all of you, you are family to me."

Lisa walked up to Sarah and handed the baby to Sarah, "Sam wants to say goodbye to you."

Sarah took Sam into her arms and gave him a little kiss on the side of his face with a little smile, "Now you listen to your mom and dad while I'm gone." She then looked at Lisa, I can hardly find the words to say thank you for helping me through everything and to too learn

about be a lady and not a slave." She then handed Sam back to Lisa and turned and giving me a big hug, "You are like a big brother to me and your wives helped teach me to laugh, even at myself. There is no way I can ever thank you and your family for everything you have done for me these last few years. You took a scared young girl into your home and made her part of your family, for that I will let you have the rest of the gold and gems to do what ever you want to with it, but please use it for good things."

I was beaming ear to ear, "I think there is enough left to build at least two more schools somewhere on one of the planets you have not build one yet, believe me when I tell you it will go to good use."

Sarah thought back and giggle a little to herself as she remembered being at some of the schools, she would on occasion feel the cold draft and she just know she was doing the right thing and that her mother was happy for her. Even when she had tried to go out with some boys, she knew that her mother was watching, too bad none of the boy ever seemed to work out for her.

Sarah wiped a small tear from her face as gave both Lisa and I another hug and then turned and walked into the shuttle. She moved into the cockpit and sat down in the captain's seat, good thing I taught her how to pilot a long time ago, then she started the engines lifted off and headed toward space, she was not sure where she was headed but she knew it would be just another adventure. She closed her eyes and reached out with her hand and set course without looking at the panel, then she just sat back and relaxed, she wished she was doing the right thing, but she also knew that she had spent a lot of time and worked hard to make the system a better place to live and it was now time to move on.

Once in space she got up and moved over to the side window and looked out at the starts as she said a small prayer that no one would come looking for her. For the past year she had fought the feeling that she needed to go somewhere and join her mother and the others as Black Ghost's.

For the next two days she just let the ship fly on autopilot she never looked at the coordinates she had set, in some ways she did not want to know. Finally curiosity got the best of her and she had to look at the panel, she saw that she was headed for Janus, it was near now and would head into its clouds soon. She had to smile at herself because she knew that soon she would be home and starting her new life as a Black Ghost. Part of her was scared and part of her excited many emotions were surfacing. For reason unknown to shuttle seems to be flying itself as it makes it way down though the clouds after she had felt that cold draft enter the cockpit.

After a few minutes she spotted the surface to the planet and saw a few small building and one large one, shuttle change course and headed forward the large one.

Once on the surface Sarah exited the shuttle and walked straight toward the larger building, the door was wide open. Once inside she spotted all of the familiar cylinders she had seen before in the cave and one of them was open. Her father's sarcophagus was up against one side of the walls. She took a deep breath and entered into the center of the room, she saw a few Black Ghost sitting at a large table and they looked to be waiting for her.

One of the Black Ghost stood up and walked over to her, she heard her mother's voice, *"My daughter we*

glad to see you, you have made your choice and have chosen to join us. You have done so much good that we are humbled. Our life is not an easy one, we must work in secret and no one can ever see our face, it would mean death to whoever would see it. We have one rule that you must understand and that is that it is okay to fall in love and leave the sisterhood to marry. Just like I did when I left to marry your father and still miss him that is way I keep him close to me."

Her mother took one step back and raised her right hand and pointed toward the open cylinder, *"Enter and you will become one of us."*

With a smile Sarah headed straight toward the cylinder and her future as a Black Ghost, once inside it closed and it started to fill up with smoke.

A few minutes later the smoke dissipated the door opened and she took a step out and found herself surrounded by all of the Black Ghosts, to her surprise to her they were no longer just in shadow, and she spotted Queen Sandy standing behind them with a large smile on her face.

Queen Sandy walked up from behind the other Black Ghosts and reached out to take Sarah's hands, "Welcome to the sisterhood of Black Ghosts, I heard you were coming here and had to be here to welcome you because I use to be the leader of Black Ghosts before I fell in love and left the sisterhood. They have voted to make you the new leader, because you are the youngest and full of life, you have done such good in the years and have helped so many people, so it is your for the taking, until you chose to leave the sisterhood, or chose someone else."

Sarah just looked around at all of the Black Ghosts and then at Queen Sandy, *"I will take the leadership role*

my fellow sisters, I will do my best to be a good leader for as long as you wish me to be."

One of the Black Ghosts took one step toward her and then dropped to one knee, *"My sister there is a young man who I have fallen in love with and would like to leave the sisterhood and see if he love me too."*

Sarah nodded her head yes and pointed toward the open cylinder, *"Go my sister and may your love be one that last a long time, never forget us and promise that our secrets are safe with you."*

Without a work the Black Ghost headed straight toward the open cylinder and it closed behind her and then filled with smoke. A few minutes later the smoke left and it its place stood a young girl about twenty-five years of age, and she had a big smile on her face, she was wearing a white robe. Once she exited the cylinder she walked up to Queen Sandy, "I hope this make you happy, I do love your son and if you approve of me, I would like to see if he wishes to spend his life with me and start a family?"

Queen Sandy put her arms around the ex-Black Ghost, "I know he will love you, all he does is talk about his favorite Ghost who is always visiting him at his store, when he needs companionship. He loves it when you sing him to sleep, all you have to do is sing and he will know it's you. He is waiting in my shuttle for you, because he was anxious to meet you face to face and yes he does want to marry you."

Sandy watched as they both turned and left the building then she turned and reached out and all of the Black Ghost joined hands. Sarah was happy that she was finely home.

THE END

OTHER BOOKS BY DANIEL DAVIS

CHANGE

IN THE NAME OF THE KING

All books are on Amazon as paperback and Kindle

CPSIA information can be obtained at www.ICGtesting.com
Printed in the USA
LVOW01s1449260215

428492LV00011B/370/P